PRINCESS PINKY AND

BOOK 7

EMILY AND CAT LARSON FIND THE HIDDEN TREASURE MAP. SECRETS OF THE PIRATES.

GABRIELL MONRO

GABRIELL MONRO

PROLOGUE

In the 6th book, Princess Pinky, Emily and Cat Larson were captured by Ogres. It happened due to the cunning plan of Witch Wilella.

Suddenly, the Dragon's army appeared to save them and in charge of the army was Emily's sister, Nelly.

Nelly become a hero and everybody was grateful to her. The old friends returned home save.

However, they did not know, that Witch Wilella prepared another cruel plan for them.

Emily and Cat Larson will face another danger in the new book. Their exciting adventures are continued…

Emily sat looking out of the bedroom window. It was rai

ning again. Emily watched the beads of rain hit the window and slowly roll down.

It was cold, wet and miserable.

Nelly turned to Emily:

"What can we do?" she asked.

"I don't know" was the reply.

Nelly looked straight at Emily and said:

“Well, let’s go to Princess Pinky. We can take Cat Larson and visit the Magic Kingdom.”

A smile appeared on Emily’s face as she look happy.

“What a wonderful idea, Nelly. Quick. Let’s find Cat Larson and go.”

They both spent some time looking for Cat Larson, but he was nowhere to be seen.

“I don’t know, where we can find him,” said Emily.

“Let’s call him and say that his dinner is ready. He always comes to eat.”

Both girls called him, but he didn’t come.

Where was Cat Larson?

The Sisters sat down looking rather sad wondering where was Cat Larson. They looked on Emily's bed and he wasn't there, they looked under Emily's bed, he wasn't there either.

They didn't have a clue where he was.

Cat Larson was in fact at Princess Pinky's Castle.

When the rain started. He had sneaked under small Emily's bed and through the magic door to the Magic Kingdom.

He thought to himself that no one would miss him, but he was wrong.

He had been missed. There was no way for Emily to call her cat from the Magic Kingdom.

She had forgotten that Princess Pinky had given her a magic whistle and if she blew it Princess Pinky and Cat Larson would hear the whistle.

Then she remembered:

"I've got a whistle. I can blow the whistle and Cat Larson will hear it. He will come home then," Emily said to Nelly.

“Go on then, blow it,” replied Nelly.

Emily blew the whistle as hard as she could, there was a very loud whistle sound and the girls ears were ringing.

Cat Larson appeared from under Emily’s bed.

"Emily, what is wrong why have you called me back?" asked Cat Larson.

"We have missed you. where have you been? We put your dinner in your special dish. It's over there waiting for you," replied Emily.

"I was at Princess Pinky's. Thank you for my dinner. Is it not a little early?" asked Cat Larson. Then both together in unison they said:

"We want you to take us to the Magic Kingdom."

They were both very excited. The girls chatted with each other:

“I wonder what adventures we will have?”

“I wonder, if the witch is being naughty.”

“Who else will be there?”

These were some of the things the girls were saying in their excited state.

Cat Larson looked at them in a puzzled sort of way. "Right," he said in his best voice to give an order.

"Let's go, Princess Pinky will be surprised," he replied to them.

The girl climbed under the bed with Cat Larson just behind. In a flash, they were standing at the end of the dark alley.

“Quick. Let’s go, so no one can see us,” Emily said.

They hurried quickly down to the end of the alley and then turned to go towards the Castle.

Sitting on a tree branch was two big black crows:

“Where are you going?” the crows asked.

“Nothing to do with you,” replied Emily.

They ran to the Castle’s gates. The crows were following behind, watching and listening.

These were Wilella’s crows. They were spying and waiting for some kind of news just so they could take it to Wilella.

However, they were out of luck, nobody said anything in front of the crows and they were very disappointed.

The crows flew to Wilella's Castle just to tell her that both Emily and Nelly were visiting princess pinky and Cat Larson was also there.

Once the crows had left, the sisters went into Princess Pinky's Castle. They were all very happy to see each other and everyone hugged each other.

The sisters asked Princess Pinky if she wanted to do anything special.

The Princess thought for a while, and then she said:

"I know. Let's go to a room in the Castle, that we use as a store room. We might find something there that we can play with," the Princess said.

The Princes led the girls down some corridors and along some tunnels. They came to a large oak door.

It was locked, but the Princess had brought the magic key with her:

"Let's open the door go inside and see what we can find," the Princess said.

Princess Pinky unlocked the door, turned the handle and slowly pushed the door open. On the other side of the door, there was a large room covered in dust and cobwebs.

Nobody had been there for a very long time. Above the door was a large spider with big round eyes.

He was watching the girls and he was wondering who they could be:

"Hello," said the spider.

The girls jumped, they never saw the spider above the door and a talking spider at that.

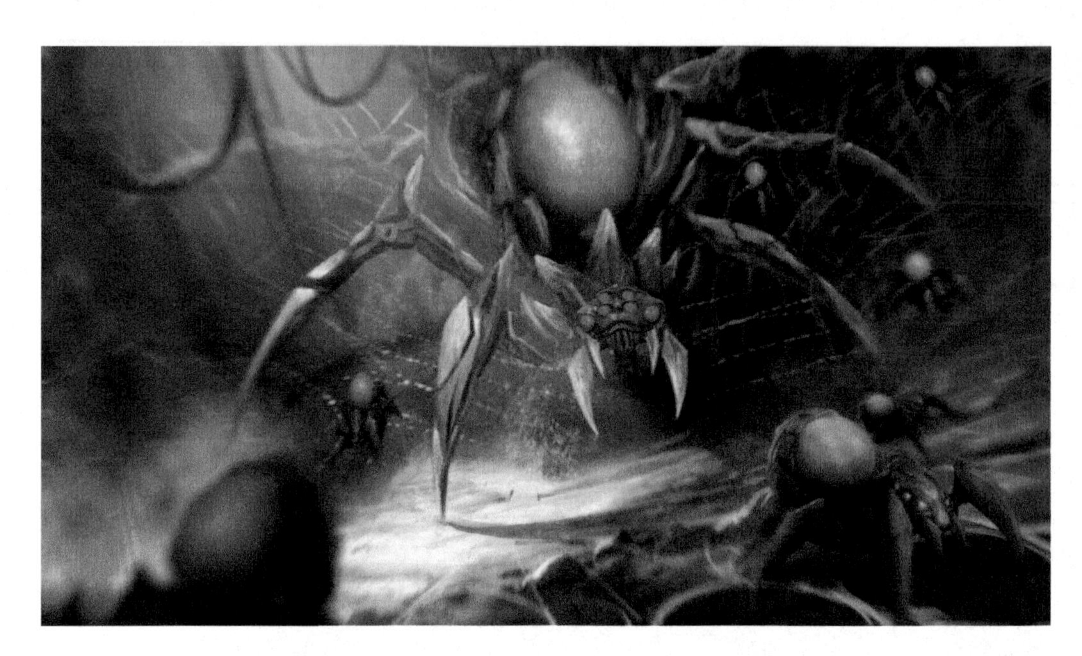

The Princess looked into the dark, and she said:

“Hello,” back.

“Who is it?” the Princess asked.

“I’m up here,” answered the spider.

The girls looked up and there in front of them was the spider.

“We didn’t see you there,” Emily said.

Nelly nodded in agreement.

“So what do we owe the pleasure of your visit?” asked the spider.

The Princess looked and said to the spider that she had heard of the room and had never been there and wanted to see what it was like, what treasures were there and if she could find anything interesting.

The girls could hear wings flapping in the darkness.

There was a family of bats hanging down from the ceiling, stretching their wings as if they were going to fly out of the hole in the window and into the night, but it was still light.

The opening of the door had awoken them and confused then about the time.

Princess Pinky looked for the light switch in the darkness, moving her hand up and down and along the wall just inside the door.

She found the switch and with a click the light came on. The girl blinked to get used to the light and they looked around the room in amazement.

There were a lot of old tables, chairs, mirrors, suits of armour, swords and shields, but in the far corner of the room half under a dirty old carpet and covered in

dust was an old treasure chest with a big padlock keeping it locked.

The girls walked across the room towards the treasure chest, moving cobwebs and blowing the dust away.

The girls held the padlock and Princess Pinky took out the magic key from her pocket. She tried it in the padlock, it fitted easily, she turned the key, and the padlock fell off the treasure chest.

Emily looked on in excitement. Nelly was smiling, they were all wondering what could be in the chest. Princess Pinky lifted the lid.

The jewels sparkled in the light, Pearls, Diamonds, Rings, Crowns and Tiaras.

In the corner was a rolled-up piece of paper. It was brown, creased and tatty looking. The Princess took out the brown paper and took it to the table.

She unrolled the paper and there in front of them was a map. It was a treasure map, the map was of the Magic Kingdom.

In a corner was a big X and Emily and Nelly both said at the same time:

“Look, it’s a treasure map and there’s the treasure,” pointing at the cross on the map.

Princess Pinky was excited about the find, then she said:

“Does everybody want to go and find the treasure?”

There was a very big loud "YES!" as everybody shouted in reply.

The Princess said:

"We need to plan our trip and there are some places to go through which are not very safe and are dangerous".

Cat Larson turned to Princess Pinky and said:

"My great great grandfather, Cat Larson Senior, told me about this map a long time ago and said it was a very tricky journey but with care, we can find the treasure."

Everybody rushed back to Princess Pinky's room.

They turned off the light, closed the door and locked it, them ran through the tunnels and corridors back.

Once inside they looked at the map again, Cat Larson said:

"We need to be careful as the Witch Wilella will be watching our every move and she will try and take the map off us."

Princess Pinky then said to everyone: "We will need to go with the Dragons and we will take Robbie the Robin as he can fly ahead and report back of anything in front of us."

Princess Pinky sent a message with the mouse to tell the Dragons that they will be going on a treasure hunt but they must not make a noise.

The mouse ran quickly over to where the Dragons lived in the Castle.

He gave the message and went back to the Princess saying they were ready whenever the treasure hunt was to begin.

The crows landed at Wilella's Castle with the news that Emily, Nelly and Cat Larson had arrived at Princess Pinky's Castle.

"I wonder, why they have turned up?" she said to herself.

"I think, I need to look into my Crystal Ball and watch these very closely," she mumbled.

Wilella took out her Crystal Ball, placing it on the table in front of her. She waved her hands and arms over the top of it. She could not see much, only fog.

Witch Wilella said the magic words:

"Oh, dear. Oh, dear, let's make it clear," slowly the fog cleared and there in front of her eyes were the sisters with Princess Pinky.

The Princess was pointing to a very special treasure chest. The chest had a very big padlock on it keeping it locked so no one could go in the chest.

Wilella was watching their every move. She saw Princess Pinky take out the magic key, unlock the padlock and open the chest.

Wilella could see all the precious things inside the chest and the map. The witch thought to herself:

“I have not seen that treasure chest since the pirates lost it a hundred years ago, so that’s where it is.

If I remember it is full of gold silver and jewels and a crumpled piece of paper,” she said to herself.

Now with Wilella seeing the chest she started to think of ways she could take the chest away from Princess Pinky and have it at her Castle.

However, it has to be done quietly. We don't want those pirates to know about the chest. But the Pirates could help her and steal the treasure map and she could find the treasure all for herself.

Back at Princess Pinky's Castle, the friends all sat around a table. They were looking at the map.

The map showed the way they needed to go, it also showed that they would travel through the forest, passed the Pirates, along the river with the

dragonflies then across the mountains and then through the swamp.

There are many tricky places they needed to go through.

As the friends started on their journey. The Unicorn came over. He wanted to go with them:

"I can carry you all on my back and we will arrive at the cross quicker," the Unicorn said.

Princess Pinky agreed and the Unicorn let the girls climb up onto his back.

The Orange giraffe was on the look out. He was looking over the Castle wall:

“All clear,” he said.

The gates opened, and the Unicorn walked through with the girls on his back. Robbie the Robin sat on Princess Pinky’s shoulder. The Dragons followed a short distance behind.

Everybody was chatting and didn’t notice the two crows watching them as they went past.

As soon as the Unicorn was out of sight, the crow took off and flew straight to Wilella's Castle. They were able to go as the crow flies the shortest route back to the witch.

They flew in through the window and landed on the back of Wilella's chair.

They told Wilella that the friends were travelling with the treasure map and that the Unicorn was taking them.

Wilella looked into her Crystal Ball. She could see them. They were heading to the forest:

"Now is the time I go to the Pirates and tell them their map has been found and Princess Pinky has it and is using it to find the Pirate treasure".

Wilella found her broomstick, sat on it and gave the instructions:

"Take me to the Pirate's village."

The broomstick rose into the air and then flew over the forest to the Pirate's village.

Wilella landed in front of the Pirate Captain's house. The Jolly Roger was flying on the flag pole above the house.

It was very quiet, there didn't seem to be anyone around.

Wilella called out: "Captain One Foot Bill, are you there?"

There was no answer, so Wilella shouted again. It was a shout that

frightened all the birds in the trees, they were scared and flew away.

Then a voice answered from inside the forest:

"Who is it?" it was Captain One Foot Bill shouting back.

“I’ve come to see you Captain One Foot Bill. I have some news that you night be interested in,” Wilella said.

“What is it?” shouted the Pirate.

"Can I come in and tell you all about it?" asked Wilella.

"Very well," said the Pirate.

They went into the Pirate's house, sitting on a perch by the window was the Captain's parrot.

It was red, yellow and Blue, the parrot spoke as they enter the room:

“Who’s this?” it said.

One Foot Bill said to Wilella to sit down by the table so she could tell him what was happening.

Wilella told the Pirate everything that the crows had told her and what she had seen in her Crystal Ball.

“Well,” said One Foot Bill. “We need to stop them and take back our pirate’s treasure map.”

Wilella smiled she did not think that the pirates would listen to her. Now they were on her side, or so she thought.

One Foot Bill called up to the crow's nest. Pirate Sam was sitting there keeping watch, but he missed the witch flying in on her broomstick.

Pirate Sam listened to the Captain, then he blew the horn calling all the pirates back to the village.

When they had all arrived, they gathered outside the Captain's house, wondering why they had been called.

"Listen, fellow Pirates. I have some news from the witch Wilella.

Our old Pirate's treasure map has been found and is in the hands of Princess Pinky.

She is using it to find our lost treasure, the treasure that was lost over one hundred years ago."

Everyone was listening intently:

"Now we need to follow the Princess and those two girls. We need to surprise them and take back our map," all the pirates cheered, clapped and laughed.

Soon they were on their way after Princess Pinky.

Wilella was so happy, now she had helped to cause trouble for Princess Pinky. She called the crows.

When they arrived, she told them to fly ahead and see where Princess Pinky was and come back with where they were. The crows left following their instructions.

Going through the forest was Princess Pinky and the girls riding on the back of the Unicorn.

The deeper they went along the track the quieter they became, everybody was looking out for anything that could surprise them, but this was difficult as it was very dark in the trees.

Everything seemed quiet. Robbie the Robin was flying ahead and flying back telling Princess Pinky what he had seen.

Robbie had not seen Wilella's crows.

They hide in the trees watching, listening and gathering necessary information ready to take it back to Wilella.

The road was slow. It was dark and cold, winding through the trees. Nobody saw a troop of monkeys swing in the trees, they were following the Princess and the friends.

The monkeys started to throw sticks at the girls and the Unicorn. The monkeys were not very good at throwing and missed every time.

The Unicorn ran fast away from the monkeys to save the girls. The Princess had thought that they had been sent by Wilella to steal the map.

They passed through the forest. In front of them was the river, the river was flowing very fast.

They walked to the bridge. This was dangerous to cross, it had holes and pieces of wood missing. It was swinging from side to side in the wind, the Unicorn said to the Princess:

“I think, it is better if I fly over to the other side.”

The Princess agreed. The Unicorn jumped and reached up and was over the river very quickly.

They walked along the path next to the river, bull-rushes lined the sides, and flying in and out of the bullrushes were hundreds of dragonflies, buzzing around the Unicorn slowing them down.

All the while the Pirates and Wilella were on the trail behind them. Chasing as fast as they could go.

One Foot Bill led the way and told them all to be quiet as the art of surprise was their best weapon.

What One Foot Bill and Wilella didn't know was the Princess's Dragons were following on behind.

On the journey continued.

Soon the Princess and Emily and Nelly passed the river and the bull rushes leaving the dragonflies behind, in front of them on the map were the mountains.

These Mountains were very high and the path up the mountains was windy, steep and slippery.

Slowly the Unicorn made his way up the path it was cold, everybody huddled together to keep warm.

Soon they were at the top, looking down at the path in front of them. They made their way down. All the time behind them were the Pirates and Wilella who were following.

Wilella had again sent the crows to see where Princess Pinky was.

They found the Unicorn and the Princess with Emily, Nelly and Cat Larson at the bottom of the mountain and heading towards the swamp. They turned around and flew back.

They told Wilella and One Foot Bill where the Princess was, One Foot Bill told everybody to speed up:

"We can catch them in the swamp and take back the map," said One Foot Bill.

The Unicorn was going slowly through the swamp as there was no path.

Soon the mud underfoot was getting very soft, and the Unicorn was sinking into the mud then the Unicorn trod into quicksand.

He began to sink, soon he was stuck in the mud, going nowhere.

The Pirates were close behind, Wilella was clapping her hands:

“We will have the map soon,” she shouted.

The Pirates and Wilella had forgotten, that they too would need to go through the swamp to catch Princess Pinky.

However, as soon as they arrived, the Pirates ran to catch the Unicorn, they sank into the mud and they were stuck.

One Foot Bill and Wilella were at the front, up to their waist in mud, sinking slowly.

The Princess looked at the map. There was no safe path through the swamp and they were stuck, but she had a plan.

She sent Robbie the Robin to fly back and get the Dragons to come to their rescue.

Robbie flew as fast as his little wings could go. He know that the Dragons were behind them and soon he found them.

He told the Dragon Master, that Princess Pinky and everyone was stuck in the swamp.

The Dragon Master gave the order and the Dragons were on their way to save the Princess and her friends.

The Dragons flew in, they stay close to the Princess who climbed onto the back of the first Dragon.

Emily and Nelly climbed onto the next Dragon. Emily held Cat Larson.

The Dragons flew to the far side of the swamp, landed and let the friend off onto dry land.

Two Dragons lifted the Unicorn out of the mud and placed him next to the Princess:

"What should we do with the Pirates and Wilella? Should we leave them in the mud?" asked the Dragon Master.

"Yes," said the Princess, "It will stop them from taking the map," Princess Pinky said.

The Princess turned to her friends:

"Quick. Let's go and follow the map and find the treasure."

The friends followed the map all the way to the cross.

The site the cross was in was an old hut in the middle of a field. There were no windows and the door was hanging off, the roof was falling in.

The Princess looked inside the hut. It was dark, dusty and covered in cobwebs.

Princess Pinky heard a voice:

"Hello, what are you doing here?"

The Princess looked up at the top of the door. Up above the Princess was a spider.

"Hello," replied the Princess.

"Have we met before?" asked Princess Pinky.

"No. We have not met before, but I have an uncle who lives in the Royal Castle.

He guards an old room inside the Castle. You may have met him," replied the spider.

"Oh, Yes, I have met him, he was a nice spider very helpful he was."

"That sounds just like my Uncle Reginald, he always tries to help everyone he meets," replied the spider.

Princess Pinky, Emily, Nelly and Cat Larson entered the hut.

The floorboards creaked. The cobwebs wobbled from side to side.

On the table in front of them was a candle holder. It had a candle in it.

Princess Pinky asks one of the Dragons to light the candle. He lit the candle and handed it to the Princess.

The room lit up, over in the far corner was a treasure chest. It was covered in dust and an old carpet.

Emily moved the carpet out of the way.

There in front of everyone was the treasure chest. This one didn't have a lock on it, it looked very old.

Nelly lifted the lid. The light from the candle made the jewels sparkle.

It was just like the treasure chest in Princess Pinky's Castle. There were all kinds of gold, silver and jewels Pearl neckless, earrings and rings.

Luckily for the Princess, the Dragons would be able to take all the treasure back to the Castle and they

would also fly on the back of the Dragons, leaving the pirates and Wilella in the mud.

Soon One Foot Bill and Wilella where shouting at each other, blaming each other as to who's fault it was that they were stuck in the mud and who was going to rescue them.

The crows circled above the arguing pair and wondered what they should do.

Wilella looked up and she shouted to the crows to fly to the witch of the south and to get her to save them.

The crows flew to the Witch of the South. They told her what had happened and that Wilella was stuck with the Pirates in the mud.

The Witch of the Sough laughed as she had never heard of a more funny story than her friend the witch Wilella being stuck.

The Witch of the South jumped onto her broomstick and followed the crows back to where Wilella and the Pirates were in the mud.

It wasn't long before the Wilella and the Pirates were rescued and they were still arguing all the way home.

Soon Princess Pinky and her friends were back at Princess Pinky's Castle. They were pleased to have found the treasure that was on the map.

The King was very happy that the map was real and there was treasure where the cross was.

Emily, Nelly and Cat Larson had had a fantastic adventure, but it was time to go back home for the sisters.

Cat Larson led the way out of the Castle and down the street to the alley.

They were back soon in Emily's bedroom.

It was still raining, then a voice from downstairs called:

"Emily, Nelly. It's tea time. Come on down and eat. what would you like to drink?"

The girls ran downstairs and into the kitchen. They sat in their seats and their mother placed their tea in front of them.

It was their favourite pizza.

Girls looked at each other with smiles and picked up the big peace from the pizza.

It was the best time of the day to be back home after dangerous adventures.

Meanwhile, their favourite friend Cat Larson just curled up on Emily's bed and went to sleep.

He had enough adventures for one day. He was dreaming about saving Emily and Nelly from Witch Wilella and he was happy about it.

He was not aware at that time, that everything that he saw in his dream at that time, will come into reality soon...

TO BE CONTINUED...

GABRIELL MONRO

DESCRIPTION

A new story "Emily and Cat Larson Find the hidden treasure map. Secrets of the Pirates" is the 7th book from the famous series of children's stories "Princess Pinky and Cat Larson". It's a very popular series across the world written by famous writer Gabriell Monro.

Gabriell Monro is one of the most popular authors. Her books are translated into 35 languages in different countries.

The famous children's book series "Princess Pinky and Cat Larson" is continued and you can read about new exciting adventures.

Princess Pinky, Emily and Cat Larson find the treasury map in the Princess Pinky's Castle. They are going to find the treasure. However, Witch Wilella and the Pirates following them to take off the treasure.

Read about their new amazing adventures…

"Exciting reading for children. My son and daughter like to read this story".

In the next book, you can read about another dark magic of Witch Wilella.

Emily and Cat Larson will face another danger in the Magic Kingdom.

They will meet with the Pirates again and finds the magic potion, which can change the appearance of the person...

GABRIELL MONRO

GABRIELL MONRO

Printed in Great Britain
by Amazon